MR. GRIGGS' WORK

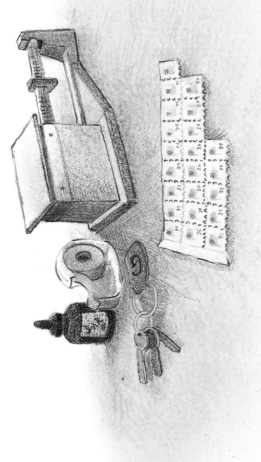

By Cynthia Rylant   Illustrated by Julie Downing

ORCHARD BOOKS · NEW YORK

A division of Franklin Watts, Inc.

Orchard Books, 387 Park Avenue South, New York, New York 10016. Orchard Books Great Britain, 10 Golden Square, London W1R 3AF England. Orchard Books Australia, 14 Mars Road, Lane Cove, New South Wales 2066. Orchard Books Canada, 20 Torbay Road, Markham, Ontario 23P 1C6. Orchard Books is a division of Franklin Watts, Inc.

Manufactured in the United States of America. Book design by Mina Greenstein.

The text of this book is set in 17 pt. Hampshire Old Style.

The illustrations are pastel drawings reproduced in full color.

10 9 8 7 6 5 4 3 2 1

Library of Congress Cataloging-in-Publication Data

Rylant, Cynthia. Mr. Griggs' work / Cynthia Rylant ; illustrations by Julie Downing.   p.   cm.

"A Richard Jackson book".— Half title p.

Summary: Mr. Griggs so loves his work at the post office that he thinks of it all the time and everything reminds him of it.

ISBN 0-531-05769-0. ISBN 0-531-08369-1 (lib. bdg.)

[1. Postal service—Fiction.   2. Occupations—Fiction.]   1. Downing, Julie, ill.   II. Title.   III. Title: Mister Griggs' work.   PZ7.R982Mr   1989   [E]—dc19   88-1484   CIP   AC

For Bill and George,
two great guys at the Kent P.O.
—C.R.

For my parents
—J.D.

Mr. Griggs worked at the old post office.

He was pretty old himself.

He had spent millions of minutes of his long life shuffling through letters, watching the pictures on the stamps change, punching his First Class puncher, weighing fat brown boxes, and listening to long tales about "The Letter That Never Got There."

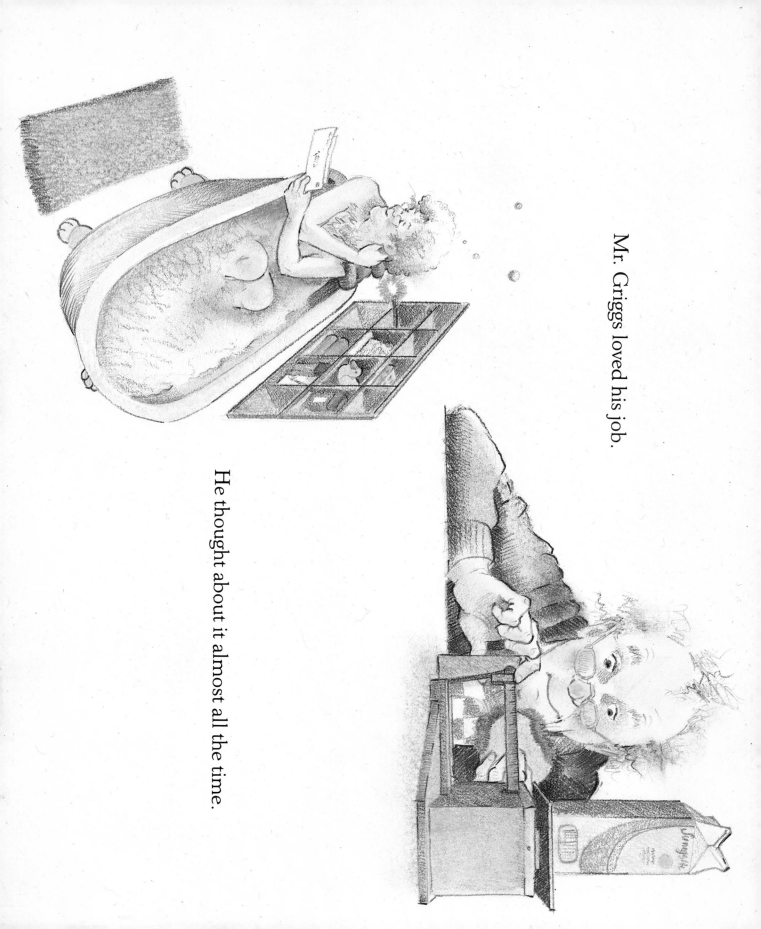

Mr. Griggs loved his job.

He thought about it almost all the time.

Now and then Mr. Griggs would be washing up his supper dishes when he'd start thinking about the fruitcake Mrs. McTacket had sent her sister fifteen Christmases ago.

That fruitcake had never arrived, and in the middle of his dishes Mr. Griggs would wonder, *Where is that fruitcake?*

Some nights he'd lie in bed wondering how much it would cost to mail a one-pound package to New Zealand or a three-ounce letter to Taiwan.

It was hard not to get up in the middle of the night and go find out. And at times, he just couldn't help himself.

Even when he went for a quiet walk in the woods, Mr. Griggs couldn't stop thinking about his work.

When a bluejay zipped over his head, he'd think: "Express Mail."

When a squirrel darted up a tree with an acorn in its mouth, he'd think: "Special Delivery."

The little holes in a rotten maple tree would remind him of his mailboxes.

He couldn't even look at a chipmunk without remembering the chipmunk stamp of 1978. But Mr. Griggs didn't mind. He loved his work.

One day Mr. Griggs became sick. His head ached and his stomach hurt and he lay in bed all day long. It was the first time he'd ever been too sick to go to work, and now someone else was taking care of his post office. Someone else was sorting through Mr. Griggs' letters, someone else was putting pennies and nickels in Mr. Griggs' drawer, someone else was taping up the corners of one of Mr. Griggs' ragged parcels.

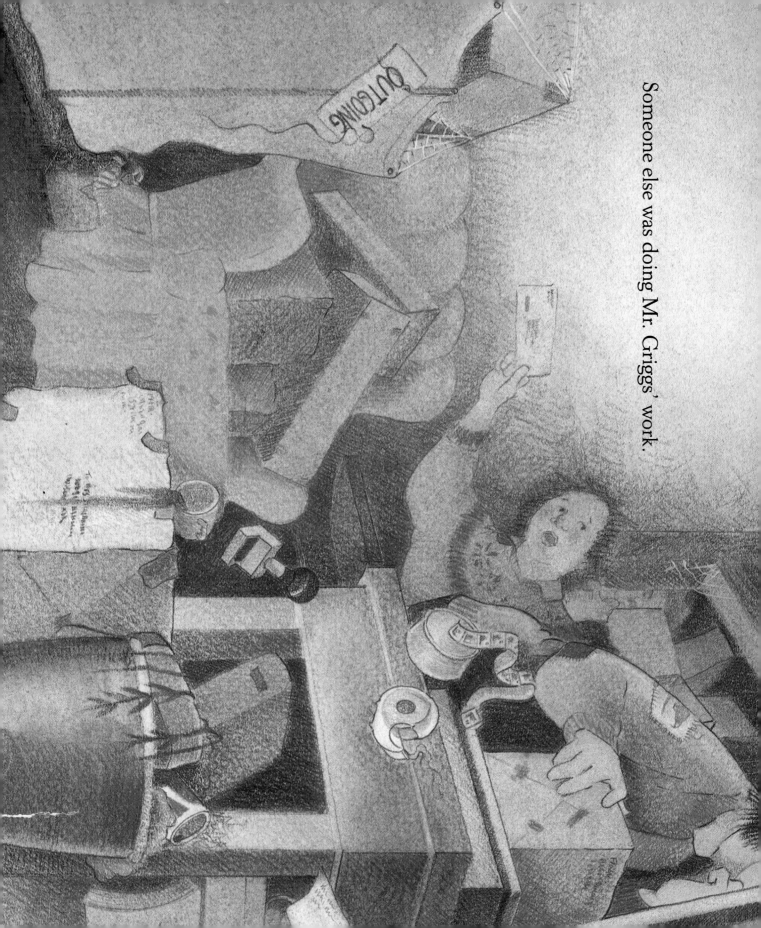

Someone else was doing Mr. Griggs' work.

Poor old Mr. Griggs felt like a dead letter.

But the next day his headache was gone
and his stomach was better.

He was still tired, though, and because he was moving slower than usual he was a little late leaving for work.

When he finally showed up at the old building, in front of it stood Mrs. Emma Bradshaw (Box 98), Mr. Frank Shrewsberry and his son Junior (Box 171), Miss Sue Ann Huckabee (Box 10), and young Bobby Bricker (Box 21).

Mr. Griggs was so glad to be back that he shook hands with them all and nearly squeezed the dickens out of young Bobby.

Then he unlocked the door of his beloved post office. He settled himself behind his little window and to Miss Huckabee, who was first in line, he said, almost gleefully, "First Class or Parcel Post?"

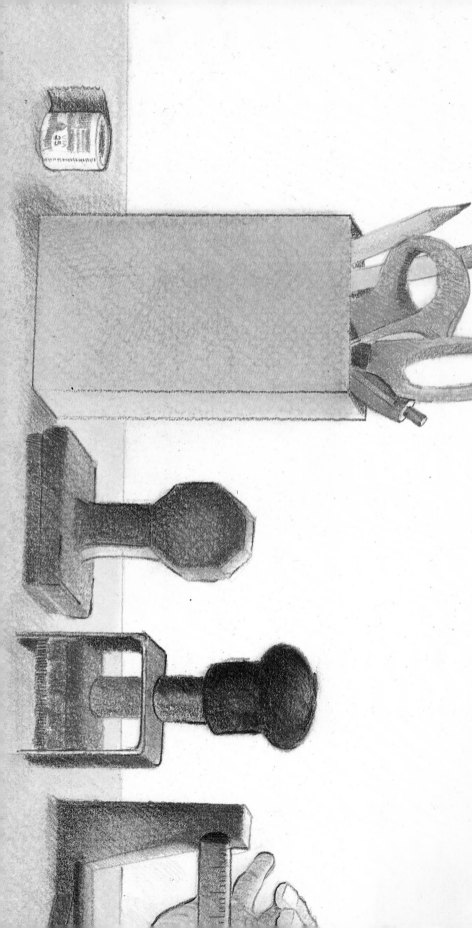

He ran his fingers over his old letter scale, he sniffed at his stamp drawer, he lined up his meters and punchers, and he glanced lovingly at all the brass mailboxes lining the walls.

In all the world that day there was nothing finer than Mr. Griggs' work.